Old MacDonald Had a Cow

Pictures by Rick Brown

Sterling Publishing Co., Inc.

New York

Library of Congress Cataloging-in-Publication Data Available

2 4 6 8 10 9 7 5 3 1

Published by Sterling Publishing Co., Inc.
387 Park Avenue South, New York, NY 10016
Text copyright © 2005 by Harriet Ziefert Inc.
Illustrations copyright © 2005 by Richard Brown
Distributed in Canada by Sterling Publishing
c/o Canadian Manda Group, 165 Dufferin Street
Toronto, Ontario, Canada M6K 3H6
Distributed in Great Britain and Europe by Chris Lloyd at Orca Book
Services, Stanley House, Fleets Lane, Poole BH15 3AJ, England
Distributed in Australia by Capricorn Link (Australia) Pty. Ltd.
P.O. Box 704, Windsor, NSW 2756, Australia

Printed in China

Sterling ISBN 1-4027-2294-X

This is Old MacDonald.

Old MacDonald had a cow.
With a moo-moo here,
And a moo-moo there,
Here a moo, there a moo,

Old MacDonald milked his cow.
With a pull-pull here,
And a pull-pull there,
Here a pull, there a pull,

Old MacDonald had a cat.
With a meow-meow here,
And a meow-meow there,
Here a meow, there a meow,

Old MacDonald had a dog.
With a bow-wow here,
And a bow-wow there,
Here a bow, there a wow,

Old MacDonald had a pony.
With a neigh-neigh here,
And a neigh-neigh there,
Here a neigh, there a neigh,

Old MacDonald had a lamb.
With a baa-baa here,
And a baa-baa there,
Here a baa, there a baa,

Old MacDonald had a piglet.
With an oink-oink here,
And an oink-oink there,
Here an oink, there an oink,

Old MacDonald had a goat.
With a mah-mah here,
And a mah-mah there,
Here a mah, there a mah,

Old MacDonald milked his cow and fed his cat, his dog, his pony, his lamb, his piglet, his goat, and his children.

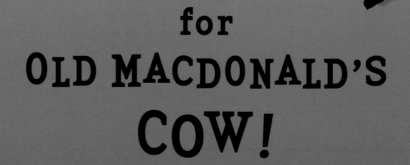

for
OLD MACDONALD'S
COW!